Stephanie Swanson

# Believe In Yourself

## Sarah's Story

AuthorHouse™
1663 Liberty Drive
Bloomington, IN 47403
www.authorhouse.com
Phone: 833-262-8899

This book is printed on acid-free paper.

ISBN: 978-1-6655-4845-8 (sc)
ISBN: 978-1-6655-4844-1 (e)
Library of Congress Control Number:     2022900361
Print information available on the last page.

Published by AuthorHouse 01/05/2022

author HOUSE

# Believe In Yourself

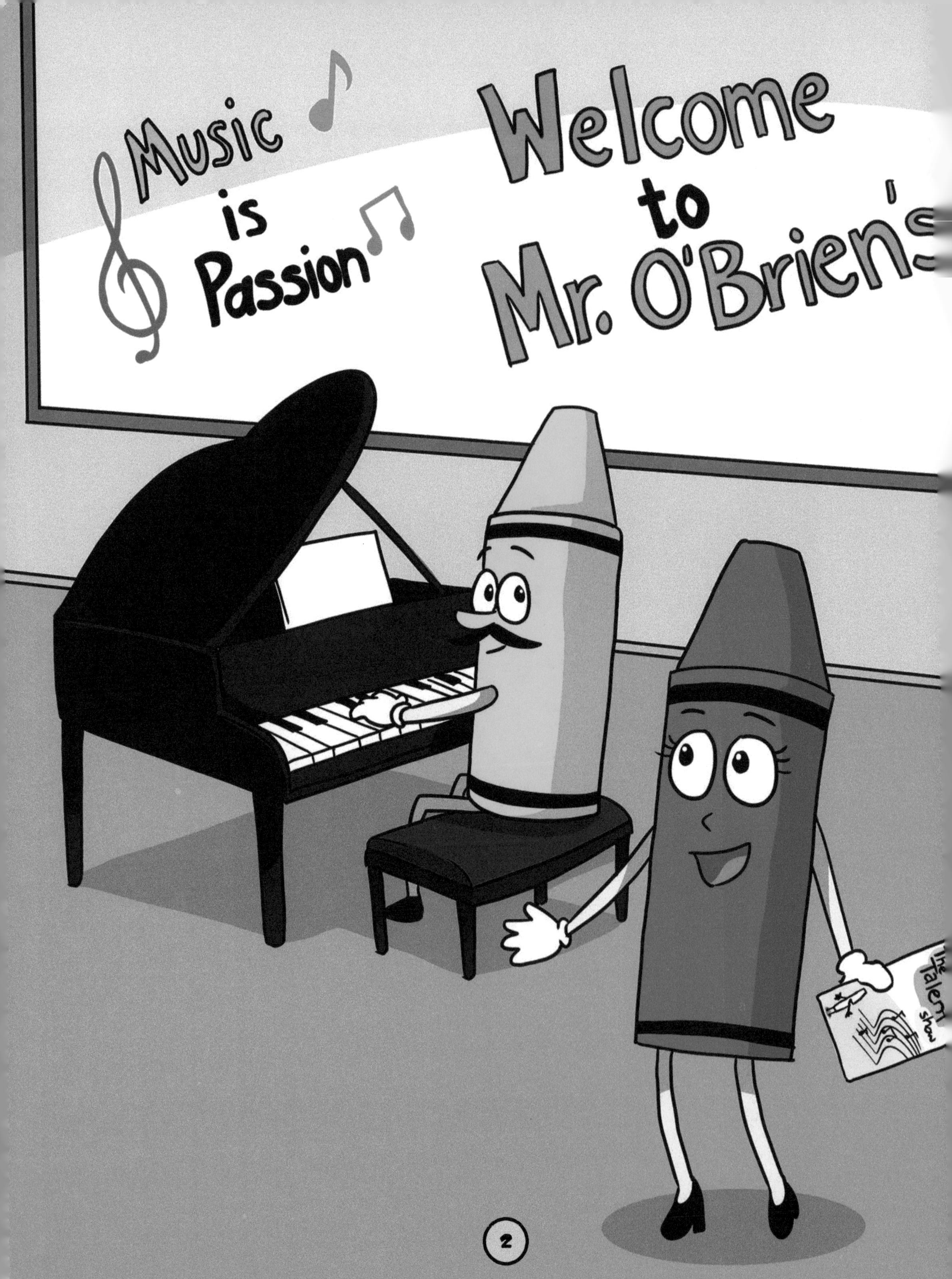
Music is Passion
Welcome to Mr. O'Brien's
The Talent show

Narrator: Sarah was a shy, non-popular kid who loved to sing and dance. But she loved to sing a little bit more than she did dance. The school's talent show was coming up in two weeks, and Sarah wanted to participate and perform her favorite song of all time. She was torn because she didn't know what people would say about her, and Sarah had stage fright. She had never performed in front of anyone besides her family and her music teacher, Mr. O'Brien. Sarah did not believe in herself.

Mr. O'Brien: Sarah, how about you participate in the school's talent show in two weeks? You are very good.

Sarah: Thank you, Mr. O'Brien, but you know that I have stage fright and have never sang in front of a crowd of people. I'm scared, and I don't think I can do it.

Mr. O'Brien: Sarah, it's not about what others think about you. It's about believing in yourself.

Sarah: I have to think about it, and I still have to ask my parents. I don't know.

Mr. O'Brien: Well, go home and speak with your parents over the weekend, and let me know what they say. I know that you can do it, and I know they know too.

Sarah: OK, thanks, Mr. O'Brien.

Narrator: Mr. O'Brien sees Sarah in the hallway on Monday and is excited to know what her parents said about the talent show.

Mr. O'Brien: Good morning, Sarah. How did the talk go with your parents?

Sarah: It went well. My parents are fine with me participating in the talent show.

Mr. O'Brien: I knew it! Are you excited?

Sarah: No, I am still nervous, and I am more worried now that Melissa will be singing as well. Everyone knows that she can sing.

Mr. O'Brien: I'll help you practice when you come to my music class. You'll be ready!

Sarah: I hope so because Melissa is really, really good!

Narrator: All week Mr. O'Brien practiced with Sarah, and every day, he was amazed. They practiced on the same stage that she would be singing on for the talent show. Sarah was scared.

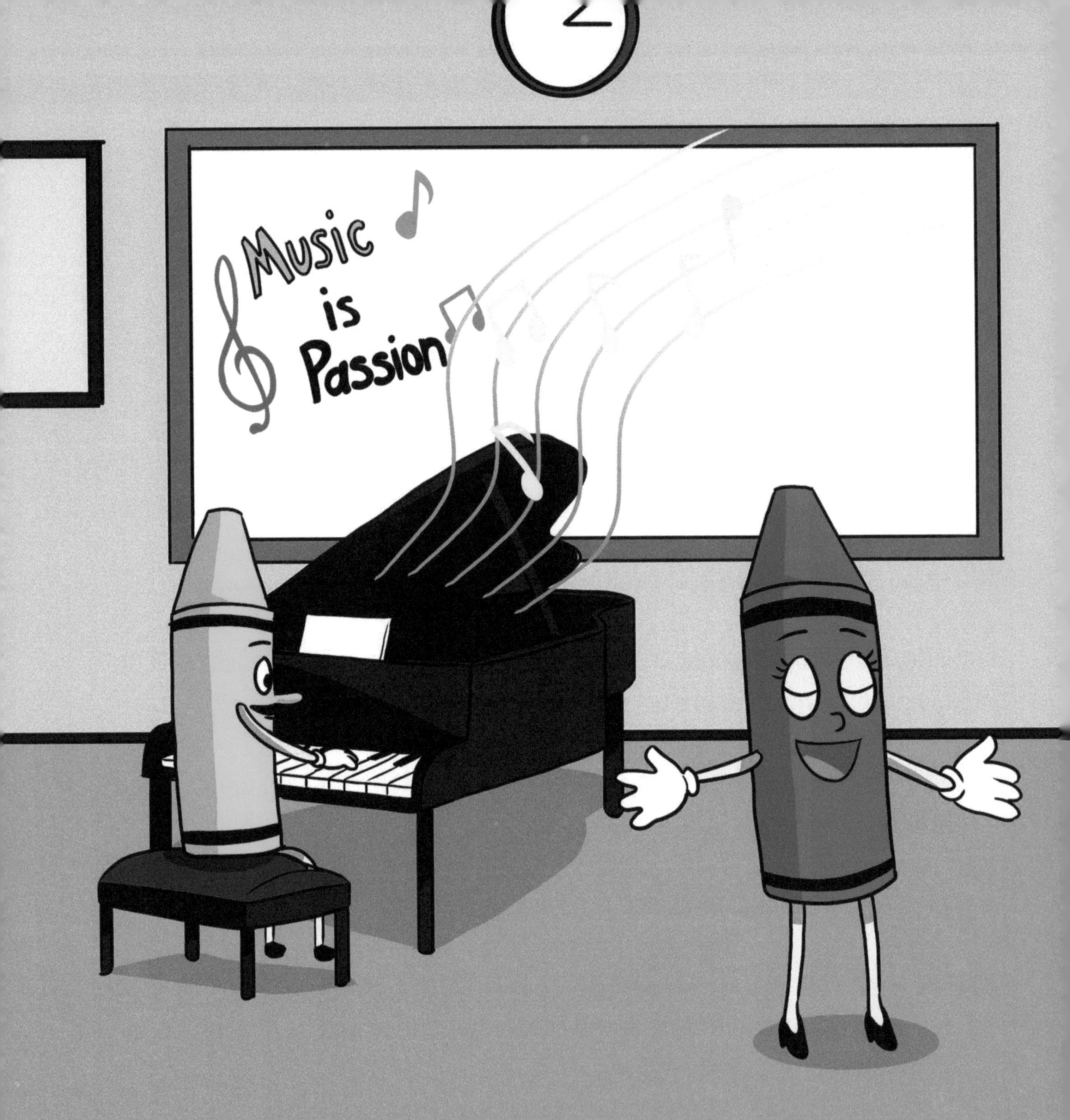
Music
is
Passion

Sarah: Mr. O'Brien, the talent show is in two days, and everybody keeps talking about how Melissa is going to beat me. I don't know about this.

Mr. O'Brien: Sarah, you have come this far, and you are doing a great job! I know that you can do this. It's not about how much better someone else can sing than you. It's about believing in yourself.

Sarah: You're right! I have worked so hard. I can't give up now. I know that I am not as popular as Melissa, but I know that I can sing. I have to believe in myself, and it starts now.

Narrator: Mr. O'Brien smiled.

Mr. O'Brien: That's it! If you believe in yourself, you can achieve anything!

Narrator: Sarah left practice that day with more confidence than she had the last two weeks. It was now talent show day, and Sarah was dressed in her favorite color, purple. She peeked out at the crowd as Melissa was singing and became nervous again. She ran back to Mr. O'Brien.

Sarah: I can't do this.

**Mr. O'Brien:** Yes, you can, Sarah! You've got me and your family cheering for you.

**Sarah:** Did you see how the crowd clapped for her?

**Mr. O'Brien:** You've got this, Sarah. Don't forget what we talked about in our practice sessions. Chin up, put a smile on your face, and sing your heart out.

**Sarah:** OK, here goes nothing.

**Narrator:** Sarah got on stage and turned into her shy phase. She didn't know if she could do it. But then she remembered the last words Mr. O'Brien spoke: "Chin up, put a smile on your face, and sing your heart out." Once the beat of her favorite song dropped, the crowd was amazed. When she noticed how the audience was into her voice, she sang harder and harder, giving the crowd everything she had. As the song finished, the entire crowd was on their feet, giving her a standing ovation. She was so surprised to have received a standing ovation. She took a bow and quickly ran off stage. Her parents were waiting for her backstage.

Sarah's mom: Aw, baby, you did so good out there singing your heart out, and it looks like the audience loved you!

Sarah's dad: We are so proud of you!

Sarah: Thanks, Mom. Thanks, Dad!

Mr. O'Brien: Where did you learn to sing like that? You were amazing!

Sarah: Well, there once was this music teacher who told me to believe in myself. I remembered those words and said that I knew I could do this. Thank you for helping me get over my stage fright!

Mr. O'Brien: You are welcome!

Narrator: Sarah learned that you must believe in yourself before anyone else can. If you know that you can do it, don't let anyone tell you anything different. Sarah took home the second-place trophy in the talent show that night, and she was so excited! She had never won anything before, and she was willing to try again next year for the first-place trophy.

The end.

CPSIA information can be obtained
at www.ICGtesting.com
Printed in the USA
BVHW011456070423
661958BV00023B/875

9 781665 548458

# THE APPLE
## DOESN'T FALL VERY FAR FROM THE
# TREE

I'm a little clumsy, just like my Poppi!

**SALVATORE PELLINGRA**

Archway Publishing books may be ordered through booksellers or by contacting:

Archway Publishing
1663 Liberty Drive
Bloomington, IN 47403
www.archwaypublishing.com
844-669-3957

ISBN: 978-1-6657-3910-8 (sc)
ISBN: 978-1-6657-3912-2 (hc)
ISBN: 978-1-6657-3911-5 (e)

Print information available on the last page.

Archway Publishing rev. date: 03/16/2023

# Foreword

As someone who grew up with ADD before it was really diagnosed, I was always doing too many things at one time resulting in all sorts of mishaps. This continued throughout my life! Running into things, forgetting, or losing personal items, getting involved in something and losing track of time. It's been a continuous source of stories for my family and friends. What I've always been able to do is laugh at what happened and use those stories to make others laugh. When my children, and now my grandchildren, are having a bad day or not feeling good or are crying from a trip or fall, I have always been able to get them to laugh their way out of their pain. One sure way to do that is a fake fall or fake bump on the head. Seeing Dad (or Poppi) trip and fall can always bring a smile to their face and take the focus off the hurt. Laughter is indeed the best medicine.

This book not only highlights bringing my grandchildren joy but also helps me see some of my traits repeating in their day to day lives. Some are so much like me, their Mimi, or their Mom or Dad. It really is a joy to see the similarities in looks, personality and actions. Along with being able to laugh after a bad experience or tough day is the comfort of seeing our family genes running through generation after generation. In a nutshell this book is about taking the pain away with laughter, knowing you aren't alone and finding comfort in knowing family bonds run deep. And most importantly, don't put so much emphasis on what others think of us or how they react to us. Don't worry about not being perfect. No one is. Enjoy the trials in life and lean in to those that love you for who you are.

# Dedication

This book is dedicated to four wonderful children, Angela, Alison, Dominic and Alexandria, now each with their own great families, and six even more amazing grandchildren, Carter, Nora, Lela, Cash, Logan and Quinn. They bring me more joy than I could ever bring them. Also, to my beautiful and compassionate wife Mary who has put up with my shenanigans for over 40 years and continues to make me a better man. I'm also grateful to God for being with me and my family every step of the way through our lifetime of adventures and for providing the blessings of grace, mercy and love to us and future generations.

Yesterday I was playing in the
park with my dog Flea.
We were having lots of fun until I
ran right into an apple tree!

## OUCH!

And then everyone started laughing...
even my dog Flea..

I ran so hard into the tree, that a
bunch of apples fell on top of me.

So many apples that I could
hardly even see.

OUCH! OUCH!

**and then some boys playing soccer ran right over me!**

# OUCH! OUCH! OUCH!

And everyone was laughing...

Even my dog Flea...

i was so embarrassed i shook myself
free and started running toward
my house on orchard Street.
But then i tripped on the curb and
fell flat on the concrete...

OUCH! OUCH! OUCH! OUCH!

When I got to my house and swung
open the door, the handle came off
and I fell "plop" right on the floor!

As I fell to the floor the door hit my back.

I was pretty sure I heard a bone crack.

## OUCH! OUCH! OUCH! OUCH! OUCH!

And everyone was laughing...
even my dog Flea!

And then I saw my Poppi
with his curly gray hair.

He picked me up from the floor
and held me right there.

Then he started walking but tripped on a stair and as he tried not to fall down, walked right into a chair!

**OUCH! OUCH! OUCH! OUCH! OUCH! OUCH!**

And then everyone started laughing...even my dog Flea, and my Poppi...

and... even... ME!!

Then my Poppi smiled and said "Gianni, the apple doesn't fall very far from the tree".

I asked "What does that mean?"

Poppi said, that's what makes you, just.... like.... me!

**So now when I am clumsy,**
**I'm happy to be.**

**It reminds me that I'm**
**just like my Poppi....**

**because the apple doesn't fall
very far from the tree!**

# About The Author

Salvatore Pellingra is an innovator who holds more than twenty-five US patents. He enjoys using his creative talents and storytelling skills to relate to others especially his children and grandchildren.

CPSIA information can be obtained
at www.ICGtesting.com
Printed in the USA
BVHW011456070423
661958BV00023B/876

9 781665 739108